Dover
CHILDREN'S THRIFT CLASSICS

Favorite
Celtic Fairy Tales

JOSEPH JACOBS

Illustrated by Thea Kliros

DOVER PUBLICATIONS, INC.
New York

DOVER CHILDREN'S THRIFT CLASSICS
EDITOR OF THIS VOLUME: CANDACE WARD

Copyright

Published in Canada by General Publishing Company, Ltd., 30 Lesmill Road, Don Mills, Toronto, Ontario.

Bibliographical Note

This Dover edition, first published in 1994, is a new selection of eight unabridged tales from *Celtic Fairy Tales* (London: David Nutt, 1891 [Dover reprint edition 0-486-21826-0]; "The Shepherd of Myddvai," "The Story of Deirdre," "The Sea-Maiden," "Beth Gellert," "The Tale of Ivan") and *More Celtic Fairy Tales* (London: David Nutt, 1894 [Dover reprint edition 0-486-21827-9]; "The Fate of the Children of Lir," "Morraha"), both collected and edited by Joseph Jacobs; "The Llanfabon Changeling" is from *The Welsh Fairy Book* by W. Jenkyn Thomas (London: Unwin, 1907). The illustrations and introductory Note have been specially prepared for this edition, and some explanatory notes have been added.

Library of Congress Cataloging-in-Publication Data

Favorite Celtic fairy tales / [selected by] Joseph Jacobs ; illustrated by Thea Kliros.
    p.   cm. — (Dover children's thrift classics)
    Contents: The fate of the children of Lir — The tale of Ivan — The shepherd of Myddvai — Morraha — The story of Deirdre — The Llanfabon changeling — Beth Gellert — The sea-maiden.
    ISBN 0-486-28352-6 (pbk.)
    1. Fairy tales—Great Britain. 2. Celts—Folklore. 3. Tales—Great Britain. [1. Fairy tales. 2. Celts—Folklore. 3. Folklore—Great Britain.] I. Jacobs, Joseph, 1854–1916. II. Kliros, Thea, ill. III. Series.
PZ8.F277   1994
398.2'089916—dc20
                                 94-37230
                                     CIP
                                     AC

Manufactured in the United States of America
Dover Publications, Inc., 31 East 2nd Street, Mineola, N.Y. 11501

Note

When noted folklorist Joseph Jacobs (1854–1916) set about to present a collection of Celtic fairy tales adapted for English children, he confessed that his main trouble was "one of selection." From a rich folklore tradition in Ireland, Scotland, Wales and Cornwall, Jacobs collected material for not only one, but two, volumes of Celtic tales, *Celtic Fairy Tales* (1891) and *More Celtic Fairy Tales* (1894). The eight tales here reflect Jacobs's efforts to include at least one tale traced to each of the four Celtic nations in the British Isles and reflecting the oral traditions of those countries.

By Jacobs's account, four of the tales ("The Sea-Maiden," "Morraha," "The Story of Deirdre" and "The Fate of the Children of Lir") are common to both Erin (Ireland) and Alba (Scotland); the two latter tales traditionally are included among the "Three Sorrowful Tales of Erin." "The Tale of Ivan" is from Cornwall, a nineteenth-century translation of a Cornish version transcribed in 1707. There are three Welsh tales: "The Shepherd of Myddvai," "The Llanfabon Changeling" and "Beth Gellert."

The last, a fable of a loyal dog killed by its master,

is perhaps the best example of legend's influence on actual history. While the literal route of the cautionary story—a warning against rash action—can be traced from sources in India, through England via the Crusades and then to Wales, Welsh tradition has given the anonymous dog the name of Gellert, Prince Llewelyn's famous greyhound. The legend became so deeply embedded in Welsh culture that in a fifteenth-century heraldry roll, the national crest of Wales was described as having the figure of a greyhound in a cradle resting on a coronet. In 1794, the story of Llewelyn and his dog was told in a collection of Welsh ballads, with a note describing the story as "traditionary in a village at the foot of Snowdon where Llewelyn the Great had a house. The Greyhound named Gêlert was given to him by his father-in-law, King John, in 1205, and the place to this day is called Beth-Gêlert, or the grave of Gêlert." The village of Bedd Gêlert was actually named for an Augustinian abbey there, Beth Kellarth. But by the end of the eighteenth century, the public had so embraced this now localized legend that an innkeeper, beset by tourists looking for the dog's grave, provided one by laying the cairn!

Contents

List of Illustrations

The Fate of the Children of Lir

IT HAPPENED that the five Kings of Ireland met to determine who should have the head kingship over them, and King Lir of the Hill of the White Field expected surely he would be elected. When the nobles went into council together they chose for head king, Dearg, son of Daghda, because his father had been so great a Druid and he was the eldest of his father's sons. But Lir left the Assembly of the Kings and went home to the Hill of the White Field. The other kings would have followed after Lir to give him wounds of spear and wounds of sword for not yielding obedience to the man to whom they had given the over-lordship. But Dearg the king would not hear of it and said: "Rather let us bind him to us by the bonds of kinship, so that peace may dwell in the land. Send over to him for wife the choice of the three maidens of the fairest form and best repute in Erin [Ireland], the three daughters of Oilell of Aran, my own three bosom-nurslings."

So the messengers brought word to Lir that Dearg the king would give him a foster-child of his foster-children. Lir thought well of it, and set out next day with fifty chariots from the Hill of the White Field. And he came to the Lake of the Red Eye near Killaloe. And when Lir saw the three daughters of Oilell, Dearg

1

the king said to him: "Take thy choice of the maidens, Lir." "I know not," said Lir, "which is the choicest of them all; but the eldest of them is the noblest; it is she I had best take." "If so," said Dearg the king, "Ove is the eldest, and she shall be given to thee, if thou willest." So Lir and Ove were married and went back to the Hill of the White Field.

And after this there came to them twins, a son and a daughter, and they gave them for names Fingula and Aod. And two more sons came to them, Fiachra and Conn. When they came Ove died, and Lir mourned bitterly for her, and but for his great love for his children he would have died of his grief. And Dearg the king grieved for Lir and sent to him and said: "We grieve for Ove for thy sake; but, that our friendship may not be rent asunder, I will give unto thee her sister, Oifa, for a wife." So Lir agreed, and they were united, and he took her with him to his own house. And at first Oifa felt affection and honour for the children of Lir and her sister, and indeed every one who saw the four children could not help giving them the love of his soul. Lir doted upon the children, and they always slept in beds in front of their father. But thereupon the dart of jealousy passed into Oifa on account of this and she came to regard the children with hatred and enmity. One day her chariot was yoked for her and she took with her the four children of Lir in it. Fingula was not willing to go with her on the journey, for she had dreamed a dream in the night warning her against Oifa: but she was not to

avoid her fate. And when the chariot came to the
Lake of the Oaks, Oifa said to the people: "Kill the
four children of Lir and I will give you your own
reward of every kind in the world." But they refused
and told her it was an evil thought she had. Then she
would have raised a sword herself to kill and destroy
the children, but her own womanhood and her weakness prevented her; so she drove the children of Lir
into the lake to bathe, and they did as Oifa told them.
As soon as they were upon the lake she struck them
with a Druid's wand of spells and wizardry and put
them into the forms of four beautiful, perfectly white
swans, and she sang this song over them:

"Out with you upon the wild waves, children of the king!
Henceforth your cries shall be with the flocks of birds."

And Fingula answered:

"Thou witch! we know thee by thy right name!
Thou mayest drive us from wave to wave,
But sometimes we shall rest on the headlands;
We shall receive relief, but thou punishment.
Though our bodies may be upon the lake,
Our minds at least shall fly homewards."

And again she spoke: "Assign an end for the ruin
and woe which thou hast brought upon us."

Oifa laughed and said: "Never shall ye be free until
the woman from the south be united to the man from
the north, until Lairgnen of Connaught wed Deoch of

She struck them with a Druid's wand of spells and wizardry and put them into the forms of four beautiful, perfectly white swans.

Munster; nor shall any have power to bring you out of these forms. Nine hundred years shall you wander over the lakes and streams of Erin. This only I will grant unto you: that you retain your own speech, and there shall be no music in the world equal to yours, the plaintive music you shall sing." This she said because repentance seized her for the evil she had done.

And then she spake this lay:

> "Away from me, ye children of Lir,
> Henceforth the sport of the wild winds,
> Until Lairgnen and Deoch come together,
> Until ye are on the north-west of Red Erin.

> "A sword of treachery is through the heart of Lir,
> Of Lir the mighty champion,
> Yet though I have driven a sword,
> My victory cuts me to the heart."

Then she turned her steeds and went on to the Hall of Dearg the king. The nobles of the court asked her where were the children of Lir, and Oifa said: "Lir will not trust them to Dearg the king." But Dearg thought in his own mind that the woman had played some treachery upon them, and he accordingly sent messengers to the Hall of the White Field.

Lir asked the messengers: "Wherefore are ye come?"

"To fetch thy children, Lir," said they.

"Have they not reached you with Oifa?" said Lir.

"They have not," said the messengers; "and Oifa

said it was you would not let the children go with her."

Then was Lir melancholy and sad at heart, hearing these things, for he knew that Oifa had done wrong upon his children, and he set out towards the Lake of the Red Eye. And when the children of Lir saw him coming Fingula sang the lay:

> "Welcome the cavalcade of steeds
> Approaching the Lake of the Red Eye,
> A company dread and magical
> Surely seek after us.

> "Let us move to the shore, O Aod,
> Fiachra and comely Conn,
> No host under heaven can those horsemen be
> But King Lir with his mighty household."

Now as she said this King Lir had come to the shores of the lake and heard the swans speaking with human voices. And he spake to the swans and asked them who they were. Fingula answered and said: "We are thy own children, ruined by thy wife, sister of our own mother, through her ill mind and her jealousy." "For how long is the spell to be upon you?" said Lir. "None can relieve us till the woman from the south and the man from the north come together, till Lairgnen of Connaught wed Deoch of Munster."

Then Lir and his people raised their shouts of grief, crying, and lamentation, and they stayed by the shore of the lake listening to the wild music of the swans until the swans flew away, and King Lir went on to the Hall of Dearg the king. He told Dearg the king what Oifa had done to his children. And Dearg put his power upon Oifa and bade her say what shape on earth she would think the worst of all. She said it would be in the form of an air-demon. "It is into that form I shall put you," said Dearg the king, and he struck her with a Druid's wand of spells and wizardry and put her into the form of an air-demon. And she flew away at once, and she is still an air-demon, and shall be so for ever.

But the children of Lir continued to delight the clans with the very sweet fairy music of their songs, so that no delight was ever heard in Erin to compare with their music until the time came appointed for the leaving the Lake of the Red Eye.

Then Fingula sang this parting lay:

"Farewell to thee, Dearg the king,
  Master of the all Druid's lore!
  Farewell to thee, our father dear,
  Lir of the Hill of the White Field!

"We go to pass the appointed time
  Away and apart from the haunts of men,
  In the current of the Moyle,
  Our garb shall be bitter and briny,

"Until Deoch come to Lairgnen.
  So come, ye brothers of once ruddy cheeks;
  Let us depart from this Lake of the Red Eye,
  Let us separate in sorrow from the tribe that has loved us."

And after they took to flight, flying highly, lightly, aerially till they reached the Moyle, between Erin and Albain [England].

The men of Erin were grieved at their leaving, and
it was proclaimed throughout Erin that henceforth no
swan should be killed. Then they stayed all solitary,
all alone, filled with cold and grief and regret, until a
thick tempest came upon them and Fingula said:
"Brothers, let us appoint a place to meet again if the
power of the winds separate us." And they said: "Let
us appoint to meet, O sister, at the Rock of the Seals."
Then the waves rose up and the thunder roared, the
lightnings flashed, the sweeping tempest passed over
the sea, so that the children of Lir were scattered
from each other over the great sea. There came,
however, a placid calm after the great tempest and
Fingula found herself alone, and she said this lay:

> "Woe upon me that I am alive!
> My wings are frozen to my sides.
> O beloved three, O beloved three,
> Who hid under the shelter of my feathers,
> Until the dead come back to the living,
> I and the three shall never meet again!"

And she flew to the Lake of the Seals and soon saw
Conn coming towards her with heavy step and
drenched feathers, and Fiachra also, cold and wet
and faint, and no word could they tell, so cold and
faint were they: but she nestled them under her wings
and said: "If Aod could come to us now our happi-
ness would be complete." But soon they saw Aod
coming towards them with dry head and preened
feathers: Fingula put him under the feathers of her

breast, and Fiachra under her right wing, and Conn under her left; and they made this lay:

> "Bad was our stepmother with us,
>   She played her magic on us,
>   Sending us north on the sea
>   In the shapes of magical swans.

> "Our bath upon the shore's ridge
>   Is the foam of the brine-crested tide,
>   Our share of the ale feast
>   Is the brine of the blue-crested sea."

One day they saw a splendid cavalcade of pure white steeds coming towards them, and when they came near they were the two sons of Dearg the king who had been seeking for them to give them news of Dearg the king and Lir their father. "They are well," they said, "and live together happy in all except that ye are not with them, and for not knowing where ye have gone since the day ye left the Lake of the Red Eye." "Happy are not we," said Fingula, and she sang this song:

> "Happy this night the household of Lir,
>   Abundant their meat and their wine.
>   But the children of Lir—what is their lot?
>   For bed-clothes we have our feathers,
>   And as for our food and our wine—
>   The white sand and the bitter brine,
>   Fiachra's bed and Conn's place,
>   Under the cover of my wings on the Moyle,
>   Aod has the shelter of my breast,
>   And so side by side we rest."

So the sons of Dearg the king came to the Hall of Lir and told the king the condition of his children.

Then the time came for the children of Lir to fulfil their lot, and they flew in the current of the Moyle to the Bay of Erris, and remained there till the time of their fate, and then they flew to the Hill of the White Field and found all desolate and empty, with nothing but unroofed green raths and forests of nettles—no house, no fire, no dwelling-place. The four came close together, and they raised three shouts of lamentation aloud, and Fingula sang this lay:

> "Uchone! it is bitterness to my heart
>   To see my father's place forlorn—
>   No hounds, no packs of dogs,
>   No women, and no valiant kings

> "No drinking-horns, no cups of wood,
>   No drinking in its lightsome halls.
>   Uchone! I see the state of this house,
>   That its lord our father lives no more.

> "Much have we suffered in our wandering years,
>   By winds buffeted, by cold frozen;
>   Now has come the greatest of our pain—
>   There lives no man who knoweth us in the house
>   where we were born."

So the children of Lir flew away to the Glory Isle of Brandan the saint, and they settled upon the Lake of the Birds until the holy Saint Patrick came to Erin and the holy Saint Mac Howg came to Glory Isle.

And the first night he came to the island the chil-

dren of Lir heard the voice of his bell ringing for
matins, so that they started and leaped about in terror
at hearing it; and her brothers left Fingula alone.
"What is it, beloved brothers?" said she. "We know
not what faint, fearful voice it is we have heard." Then
Fingula recited this lay:

> "Listen to the Cleric's bell,
>   Poise your wings and raise
>   Thanks to God for his coming,
>   Be grateful that you hear him.

> "He shall free you from pain,
>   And bring you from the rocks and stones.
>   Ye comely children of Lir,
>   Listen to the bell of the Cleric."

And Mac Howg came down to the brink of the
shore and said to them: "Are ye the children of Lir?"
"We are indeed," said they. "Thanks be to God!" said
the saint; "it is for your sakes I have come to this Isle
beyond every other island in Erin. Come ye to land
now and put your trust in me." So they came to land,
and he made for them chains of bright white silver,
and put a chain between Aod and Fingula and a
chain between Conn and Fiachra.

It happened at this time that Lairgnen was prince of
Connaught and he was to wed Deoch the daughter of
the king of Munster. She had heard the account of the
birds and she became filled with love and affection
for them, and she said she would not wed till she had
the wondrous birds of Glory Isle. Lairgnen sent for

them to the Saint Mac Howg. But the Saint would not give them, and both Lairgnen and Deoch went to Glory Isle. And Lairgnen went to seize the birds from the altar: but as soon as he had laid hands on them their feathery coats fell off, and the three sons of Lir became three withered bony old men, and Fingula, a lean withered old woman without blood or flesh. Lairgnen started at this and left the place hastily, but Fingula chanted this lay:

> "Come and baptise us, O Cleric,
> Clear away our stains!
> This day I see our grave—
> Fiachra and Conn on each side,
> And in my lap, between my two arms,
> Place Aod, my beauteous brother."

After this lay, the children of Lir were baptised. And they died, and were buried as Fingula had said, Fiachra and Conn on either side, and Aod before her face. A cairn [burial marker] was raised for them, and on it their names were written in runes. And that is the fate of the children of Lir.

The Tale of Ivan

THERE WERE formerly a man and a woman living in the parish of Llanlavan, in the place which is called Hwrdh. And work became scarce, so the man said to his wife, "I will go search for work, and you may live here." So he took fair leave, and travelled far toward the East, and at last came to the house of a farmer and asked for work.

"What work can ye do?" said the farmer.

"I can do all kinds of work," said Ivan.

Then they agreed upon three pounds for the year's wages.

When the end of the year came his master showed him the three pounds. "See, Ivan," said he, "here's your wage; but if you will give it me back I'll give you a piece of advice instead."

"Give me my wage," said Ivan.

"No, I'll not," said the master; "I'll explain my advice."

"Tell it me, then," said Ivan.

Then said the master, "Never leave the old road for the sake of a new one."

After that they agreed for another year at the old wages, and at the end of it Ivan took instead a piece of advice, and this was it: "Never lodge where an old man is married to a young woman."

The same thing happened at the end of the third year, when the piece of advice was: "Honesty is the best policy."

But Ivan would not stay longer, but wanted to go back to his wife.

"Don't go to-day," said his master; "my wife bakes to-morrow, and she shall make thee a cake to take home to thy good woman."

And when Ivan was going to leave, "Here," said his master, "here is a cake for thee to take home to thy wife, and, when ye are most joyous together, then break the cake, and not sooner."

So he took fair leave of them and travelled towards home, and at last he came to Wayn Her, and there he met three merchants from Tre Rhyn, of his own parish, coming home from Exeter Fair. "Oho! Ivan," said they, "come with us; glad are we to see you. Where have you been so long?"

"I have been in service," said Ivan, "and now I'm going home to my wife."

"Oh, come with us! you'll be right welcome."

But when they took the new road Ivan kept to the old one. And robbers fell upon them before they had gone far from Ivan as they were going by the fields of the houses in the meadow. They began to cry out, "Thieves!" and Ivan shouted out "Thieves!" too. And when the robbers heard Ivan's shout they ran away, and the merchants went by the new road and Ivan by the old one till they met again at Market-Jew.

"Oh, Ivan," said the merchants, "we are beholding

to you; but for you we would have been lost men. Come lodge with us at our cost, and welcome."

When they came to the place where they used to lodge, Ivan said, "I must see the host."

"The host," they cried; "what do you want with the host? Here is the hostess, and she's young and pretty. If you want to see the host you'll find him in the kitchen."

So he went into the kitchen to see the host; he found him a weak old man turning the spit.

"Oh! oh!" quoth Ivan, "I'll not lodge here, but will go next door."

"Not yet," said the merchants, "sup with us, and welcome."

Now it happened that the hostess had plotted with a certain monk in Market-Jew to murder the old man in his bed that night while the rest were asleep, and they agreed to lay it on the lodgers.

So while Ivan was in bed next door, there was a hole in the pine-end of the house, and he saw a light through it. So he got up and looked, and heard the monk speaking. "I had better cover this hole," said he, "or people in the next house may see our deeds." So he stood with his back against it while the hostess killed the old man.

But meanwhile Ivan out with his knife, and putting it through the hole, cut a round piece off the monk's robe.

The very next morning the hostess raised the cry that her husband was murdered, and as there was neither man nor child in the house but the merchants, she declared they ought to be hanged for it.

So they were taken and carried to prison, till at last Ivan came to them. "Alas! alas! Ivan," cried they, "bad luck sticks to us; our host was killed last night, and we shall be hanged for it."

"Ah, tell the justices," said Ivan, "to summon the real murderers."

"Who knows," they replied, "who committed the crime?"

"Who committed the crime!" said Ivan. "If I cannot prove who committed the crime, hang me in your stead."

So he told all he knew, and brought out the piece of cloth from the monk's robe, and with that the merchants were set at liberty, and the hostess and the monk were seized and hanged.

Then they came all together out of Market-Jew, and they said to him: "Come as far as Coed Carrn y Wylfa, the Wood of the Heap of Stones of Watching, in the parish of Burman. Then their two roads separated, and though the merchants wished Ivan to go with them, he would not go with them, but went straight home to his wife.

And when his wife saw him she said: "Home in the nick of time. Here's a purse of gold that I've found; it has no name, but sure it belongs to the great lord yonder. I was just thinking what to do when you came."

Then Ivan thought of the third counsel, and he said: "Let us go and give it to the great lord."

So they went up to the castle, but the great lord was not in it, so they left the purse with the servant that minded the gate, and then they went home again and lived in quiet for a time.

But one day the great lord stopped at their house for a drink of water, and Ivan's wife said to him: "I hope your lordship found your lordship's purse quite safe with all its money in it."

"What purse is that you are talking about?" said the lord.

"Sure, it's your lordship's purse that I left at the castle," said Ivan.

"Come with me and we will see into the matter," said the lord.

So Ivan and his wife went up to the castle, and there they pointed out the man to whom they had given the purse, and he had to give it up and was sent away from the castle. And the lord was so pleased with Ivan that he made him his servant in the stead of the thief.

"Honesty's the best policy!" quoth Ivan, as he skipped about in his new quarters. "How joyful I am!"

Then he thought of his old master's cake that he was to eat when he was most joyful, and when he broke it, lo and behold, inside it was his wages for the three years he had been with him.

The Shepherd of Myddvai

UP IN THE Black Mountains in Caermarthenshire lies the lake known as Lyn y Van Vach. To the margin of this lake the shepherd of Myddvai once led his lambs, and lay there whilst they sought pasture. Suddenly, from the dark waters of the lake, he saw three maidens rise. Shaking the bright drops from their hair and gliding to the shore, they wandered about amongst his flock. They had more than mortal beauty, and he was filled with love for her that came nearest to him. He offered her the bread he had with him, and she took it and tried it, but then sang to him:

> Hard-baked is thy bread,
> 'Tis not easy to catch me,

and then ran off laughing to the lake.

Next day he took with him bread not so well done, and watched for the maidens. When they came ashore he offered his bread as before, and the maiden tasted it and sang:

> Unbaked is thy bread,
> I will not have thee,

and again disappeared in the waves.

Shaking the bright drops from their hair and gliding to the shore, they wandered about amongst his flock.

A third time did the shepherd of Myddvai try to attract the maiden, and this time he offered her bread that he had found floating about near the shore. This pleased her, and she promised to become his wife if he were able to pick her out from among her sisters on the following day. When the time came the shepherd knew his love by the strap of her sandal. Then she told him she would be as good a wife to him as any earthly maiden could be unless he should strike her three times without cause. Of course he deemed that this could never be; and she, summoning from the lake three cows, two oxen, and a bull, as her marriage portion, was led homeward by him as his bride.

The years passed happily, and three children were born to the shepherd and the lake-maiden. But one day there was going to be a christening, and she said to her husband it was far to walk, so he told her to go for the horses.

"I will," said she, "if you bring me my gloves which I've left in the house."

But when he came back with the gloves, he found she had not gone for the horses; so he tapped her lightly on the shoulder with the gloves, and said, "Go, go."

"That's one," said she.

Another time they were at a wedding, when suddenly the lake-maiden fell a-sobbing and a-weeping, amid the joy and mirth of all around her.

Her husband tapped her on the shoulder, and asked her, "Why do you weep?"

"Because they are entering into trouble; and trouble is upon you; for that is the second causeless blow you have given me. Be careful; the third is the last."

The husband was careful never to strike her again. But one day at a funeral she suddenly burst out into fits of laughter. Her husband forgot, and touched her rather roughly on the shoulder, saying, "Is this a time for laughter?"

"I laugh," she said, "because those that die go out of trouble, but your trouble has come. The last blow has been struck; our marriage is at an end, and so farewell." And with that she rose up and left the house and went to their home.

Then she, looking round upon her home, called to the cattle she had brought with her:

> Brindle cow, white speckled,
> Spotted cow, bold freckled,
> Old white face, and gray Geringer,
> And the white bull from the king's coast,
> Grey ox, and black calf,
> All, all, follow me home.

Now the black calf had just been slaughtered, and was hanging on the meat hook; but it got off the hook alive and well and followed her; and the oxen, though they were ploughing, trailed the plough with them and did her bidding. So she fled to the lake again, they following her, and with them plunged into the dark waters. And to this day is the furrow seen which the plough left as it was dragged across the mountains to the tarn [lake].

Only once did she come again, when her sons were grown to manhood, and then she gave them gifts of healing by which they won the name of Meddygon Myddvai, the physicians of Myddvai.

Morraha

MORRAHA ROSE in the morning and washed his hands and face, and said his prayers, and ate his food; and he asked God to prosper the day for him. So he went down to the brink of the sea, and he saw a currach [small boat], short and green, coming towards him; and in it there was but one youthful champion, and he was playing hurly [a game like hockey] from prow to stern of the currach. He had a hurl [stick] of gold and a ball of silver; and he stopped not till the currach was in on the shore; and he drew her up on the green grass, and put fastenings on her for a year and a day, whether he should be there all that time or should only be on land for an hour by the clock. And Morraha saluted the young man courteously; and the other saluted him in the same fashion, and asked him would he play a game of cards with him; and Morraha said that he had not the wherewithal; and the other answered that he was never without a candle or the making of it; and he put his hand in his pocket and drew out a table and two chairs and a pack of cards, and they sat down on the chairs and went to card-playing. The first game Morraha won, and the Slender Red Champion bade him make his claim; and he asked that the land above him should be filled with sheep in the morning. It was well; and he played no second game, but home he went.

The next day Morraha went to the brink of the sea, and the young man came in the currach and asked him would he play cards; they played, and Morraha won. The young man bade him make his claim; and he asked that the land above should be filled with cattle in the morning. It was well; and he played no other game, but went home.

On the third morning Morraha went to the brink of the sea, and he saw the young man coming. He drew up his boat on the shore and asked him would he play cards. They played, and Morraha won the game; and the young man bade him give his claim. And he said he would have a castle and a wife, the finest and fairest in the world; and they were his. It was well; and the Red Champion went away.

On the fourth day his wife asked him how he had found her. And he told her. "And I am going out," said he, "to play again to-day."

"I forbid you to go again to him. If you have won so much, you will lose more; have no more to do with him."

But he went against her will, and he saw the currach coming; and the Red Champion was driving his balls from end to end of the currach; he had balls of silver and a hurl of gold, and he stopped not till he drew his boat on the shore, and make her fast for a year and a day. Morraha and he saluted each other;

and he asked Morraha if he would play a game of cards, and they played, and he won. Morraha said to him, "Give your claim now."

Said he, "You will hear it too soon. I lay on you bonds of the art of the Druid, not to sleep two nights in one house, nor finish a second meal at the one table, till you bring me the sword of light and news of the death of Anshgayliacht."

Morraha went home to his wife and sat down in a chair, and gave a groan, and the chair broke in pieces.

"That is the groan of the son of a king under spells," said his wife; "and you had better have taken my counsel than that the spells should be on you."

He told her he had to bring news of the death of Anshgayliacht and the sword of light to the Slender Red Champion.

"Go out," said she, "in the morning of the morrow, and take the bridle in the window, and shake it; and whatever beast, handsome or ugly, puts its head in it, take that one with you. Do not speak a word to her till she speaks to you; and take with you three pint bottles of ale and three sixpenny loaves, and do the thing she tells you; and when she runs to my father's land, on a height above the castle, she will shake herself, and the bells will ring, and my father will say, 'Brown Allree is in the land. And if the son of a king or queen is there, bring him to me on your shoulders; but if it is the son of a poor man, let him come no further.'"

He rose in the morning, and took the bridle that was in the window, and went out and shook it; and Brown Allree came and put her head in it. He took the three loaves and three bottles of ale, and went riding; and when he was riding she bent her head down to take hold of her feet with her mouth, in hopes he would speak in ignorance; but he spoke not a word during the time, and the mare at last spoke to him, and told him to dismount and give her her dinner. He gave her the sixpenny loaf toasted, and a bottle of ale to drink.

"Sit up now riding, and take good heed of yourself: there are three miles of fire I have to clear at a leap."

She cleared the three miles of fire at a leap, and asked if he were still riding, and he said he was. Then they went on, and she told him to dismount and give her a meal; and he did so, and gave her a sixpenny loaf and a bottle; she consumed them and said to him there were before them three miles of hill covered with steel thistles, and that she must clear it. She cleared the hill with a leap, and she asked him if he were still riding, and he said he was. They went on, and she went not far before she told him to give her a meal, and he gave her the bread and the bottle. She went over three miles of sea with a leap, and she came then to the land of the King of France; she went up on a height above the castle, and she shook herself and neighed, and the bells rang; and the king said that it was Brown Allree was in the land.

"Go out," said he; "and if it is the son of a king or

queen, carry him in on your shoulders; if it is not, leave him there."

They went out; and the stars of the son of a king were on Morraha's breast; they lifted him high on their shoulders and bore him in to the king. They passed the night cheerfully, playing and drinking, with sport and with diversion, till the whiteness of the day came upon the morrow morning.

Then the young king told the cause of his journey, and he asked the queen to give him counsel and good luck, and she told him everything he was to do.

"Go now," said she, "and take with you the best mare in the stable, and go to the door of Rough Niall of the Speckled Rock, and knock, and call on him to give you news of the death of Anshgayliacht and the sword of light: and let the horse's back be to the door, and apply the spurs, and away with you."

In the morning he did so, and he took the best horse from the stable and rode to the door of Niall, and turned the horse's back to the door, and demanded news of the death of Anshgayliacht and the sword of light; then he applied the spurs, and away with him. Niall followed him hard, and, as he was passing the gate, cut the horse in two. His wife was there with a dish of puddings and flesh, and she threw it in his eyes and blinded him, and said, "Fool! whatever kind of man it is that's mocking you, isn't that a fine condition you have got your father's horse into?"

On the morning of the next day Morraha rose, and

took another horse from the stable, and went again to the door of Niall, and knocked and demanded news of the death of Anshgayliacht and the sword of light, and applied the spurs to the horse and away with him. Niall followed, and as Morraha was passing the gate, cut the horse in two and took half the saddle with him; but his wife met him and threw flesh in his eyes and blinded him.

On the third day, Morraha went again to the door of Niall; and Niall followed him, and as he was passing the gate, cut away the saddle from under him and the clothes from his back. Then his wife said to Niall:

"The fool that's mocking you, is the Slender Red Champion, in the little currach; take good heed to yourself, and don't sleep one wink for three days."

After three days Niall's wife came to him and said:

"Sleep as much as you want now. He is gone."

He went to sleep, and there was heavy sleep on him, and Morraha went in and took hold of the sword that was on the bed at his head. And the sword tried to draw itself out of the hand of Morraha; but it failed. Then it gave a cry, and it wakened Niall, and Niall said it was a rude and rough thing to come into his house like that; and said Morraha to him:

"Leave your talking, or I will cut the head off you. Tell me the news of the death of Anshgayliacht."

"Oh, you can have my head."

"But your head is no good to me; tell me the story."

"Oh," said Niall's wife, "you must get the story."

"Well," said Niall, "let us sit down together till I tell

the story. I thought no one would ever get it; but now it will be heard by all."

The Story

When I was growing up, my mother taught me the language of the birds; and when I got married, I used to be listening to their conversation; and I would be laughing; and my wife would be asking me what was the reason of my laughing, but I did not like to tell her, as women are always asking questions. We went out walking one fine morning, and the birds were arguing with one another. One of them said to another:

"Why should you be comparing yourself with me, when there is not a king nor knight that does not come to look at my tree?"

"What advantage has your tree over mine, on which there are three rods [sticks] of magic mastery growing?"

When I heard them arguing, and knew that the rods were there, I began to laugh.

"Oh," asked my wife, "why are you always laughing? I believe it is at myself you are jesting, and I'll walk with you no more."

"Oh, it is not about you I am laughing. It is because I understand the language of the birds."

Then I had to tell her what the birds were saying to one another; and she was greatly delighted, and she asked me to go home, and she gave orders to the cook to have breakfast ready at six o'clock in the morning. I did not know why she was going out early, and breakfast was ready in the morning at the hour she appointed. She asked me to go out walking. I went with her. She went to the tree, and asked me to cut a rod for her.

"Oh, I will not cut it. Are we not better without it?"

"I will not leave this until I get the rod, to see if there is any good in it."

I cut the rod and gave it to her. She turned from me and struck a blow on a stone, and changed it; and she struck a second blow on me, and made of me a black raven, and she went home and left me after her. I thought she would come back; she did not come, and I had to go into a tree till morning. In the morning, at six o'clock, there was a bellman out, proclaiming that every one who killed a raven would get a fourpenny-bit. At last you could not find man or boy without a gun, nor, if you were to walk three miles, a raven that was not killed. I had to make a nest in the top of the parlour chimney, and hide myself all day till night came, and go out to pick up a bit of food to support me, till I spent a month. Here she is herself to say if it is a lie I am telling.

"It is not," said she.

Then I saw her out walking. I went up to her, and I thought she would turn me back to my own shape, and she struck me with the rod and made of me an old white horse, and she ordered me to be put to a cart with a man, to draw stones from morning till night. I was worse off then. She spread abroad a report that I had died suddenly in my bed, and prepared a coffin, and held a wake and buried me. Then she had no trouble. But when I got tired I began to kill every one who came near me, and I used to go into the haggard [stackyard] every night and destroy the stacks of corn; and when a man came near me in the morning I would follow him till I broke his bones. Every one got afraid of me. When she saw I was doing mischief she came to meet me, and I thought she would change me. And she did change me, and made a fox of me. When I saw she was doing me every sort of damage I went away from her. I knew there was a badger's hole in the garden, and I went there till night came, and I made great slaughter among the geese and ducks. There she is herself to say if I am telling a lie.

"Oh! you are telling nothing but the truth, only less than the truth."

When she had enough of my killing the fowl she came out into the garden, for she knew I was in the badger's hole. She came to me and made me a wolf. I had to be off, and go to an island, where no one at all would see me, and now and then I used to be killing sheep, for there were not many of them, and I was afraid of being seen and hunted; and so I passed a year, till a shepherd saw me among the sheep and a pursuit was made after me. And when the dogs came near me there was no place for me to escape to from them; but I recognised the sign of the king among the men, and I made for him, and the king cried out to stop the hounds. I took a leap upon the front of the king's saddle, and the woman behind cried out, "My king and my lord, kill him, or he will kill you!"

"Oh! he will not kill me. He knew me; he must be pardoned."

The king took me home with him, and gave orders I should be well cared for. I was so wise, when I got food, I would not eat one morsel until I got a knife and fork. The man told the king, and the king came to see if it was true, and I got a knife and fork, and I took the knife in one paw and the fork in the other, and I bowed to the king. The king gave orders to bring him drink, and it came; and the king filled a glass of wine and gave it to me.

I took hold of it in my paw and drank it, and thanked the king.

"On my honour," said he, "it is some king or other has lost him, when he came on the island; and I will keep him, as he is trained; and perhaps he will serve us yet."

And this is the sort of king he was,—a king who had not a child living. Eight sons were born to him and three daughters, and they were stolen the same night they were born. No matter what guard was placed over them, the child would be gone in the morning. A twelfth child now came to the queen, and the king took me with him to watch the baby. The women were not pleased.

"Oh," said the king, "what was all your watching ever good for? I have not one child that was born to me; I will leave this one in the dog's care, and he will not let it go."

A chain was put between me and the cradle, and when every one went to sleep I was watching till the person woke who attended in the daytime; but I was there only two nights; when it was near the day, I saw a hand coming down through the chimney, and the hand was so big that it took round the child altogether, and thought to take him away. I caught hold of the hand above the wrist, and as I was fastened to the cradle, I did not let go my hold till I cut the hand from the wrist, and there was a howl from the person without. I laid the hand in the cradle with the child, and as I was tired I fell asleep; and when I awoke, I had neither child nor hand; and I began to howl, and the king heard me, and he cried out that something was wrong with me, and he sent servants to see what was the matter with me, and when the messenger came he saw me covered with blood, and he could not see the child; and he went to the king and told him the child was not to be found. The king came and saw the cradle coloured with the blood, and he cried out "where was the child gone?" and every one said it was the dog had eaten it.

The king said: "It is not: loose him, and he will get the pursuit himself."

When I was loosed, I found the scent of the blood till I came to a door of the room in which the child

A chain was put between me and the cradle, and when every one went to sleep I was watching till the person woke who attended in the daytime.

was. I went back to the king and took hold of him,
and went back again and began to tear at the door.
The king followed me and asked for the key. The
servant said it was in the room of a strange woman
who lived in the castle. The king caused search to be
made for her, and she was not to be found. "I will
break the door," said the king, "as I can't get the key."
The king broke the door, and I went in, and went to
the trunk, and the king asked for a key to unlock it.
He got no key, and he broke the lock. When he
opened the trunk, the child and the hand were
stretched side by side, and the child was asleep. The
king took the hand and ordered a woman to come for
the child, and he showed the hand to every one in the
house. But the stranger woman was gone, and she
did not see the king;—and here she is herself to say if
I am telling lies of her.

"Oh, it's nothing but the truth you have!"

The king did not allow me to be tied any more. He
said there was nothing so much to wonder at as that I
cut the hand off, though I was tied.

The child was growing till he was a year old. He
was beginning to walk, and no one cared for him
more than I did. He was growing till he was three,
and he was running out every minute; so the king
ordered a silver chain to be put between me and the
child, that he might not go away from me. I was out
with him in the garden every day, and the king was as
proud as the world of the child. He would be watching him everywhere we went, till the child grew so

wise that he would loose the chain and get off. But one day that he loosed it, I failed to find him; and I ran into the house and searched the house, but there was no finding him. The king cried to go out and find the child, that had got loose from the dog. They went searching for him, but could not find him. When they failed altogether to find him, there remained no more favour with the king towards me, and every one disliked me, and I grew weak, for I did not get a morsel to eat half the time. When summer came, I said I would try and go home to my own country. I went away one fine morning, and God helped me till I came home. I went into the garden, for I knew there was a place in the garden where I could hide myself, for fear my wife should see me. In the morning I saw her out walking, and there was the child with her, held by the hand. I pushed out to see the child, and as he was looking about him everywhere, he saw me and called out, "I see my shaggy papa. Oh!" said he; "oh, my heart's love, my shaggy papa, come here till I see you!"

I was afraid the woman would see me, as she was asking the child where he saw me, and he said I was up in a tree; and the more the child called me, the more I hid myself. The woman took the child back inside with her, but I knew he would be up early in the morning.

I went to the parlour-window, and the child was within, and he playing. When he saw me he cried out, "Oh! my heart's love, come here till I see you, shaggy

papa." I broke the window and went in, and he began
to kiss me. I saw the rod in front of the chimney, and
I jumped up at the rod and knocked it down. "Oh! my
heart's love, no one would give me the pretty rod,"
said he. I hoped he would strike me with the rod, but
he did not. When I saw the time was short I raised my
paw, and I gave him a scratch below the knee. "Oh!
you naughty, dirty, shaggy papa, you have hurt me so
much, I'll give you a blow of the rod." He struck me a
light blow, and so I came back to my own shape
again. When he saw a man standing before him he
gave a cry, and I took him up in my arms. The
servants heard the child. A maid came in to see what
was the matter with him. When she saw me she gave
a cry out of her, and she said, "Oh, if the master isn't
come to life again!"

Another came in, and said it was he really. When
the mistress heard of it, she came to see with her
own eyes, for she would not believe I was there; and
when she saw me she said she'd drown herself. But I
said to her, "If you yourself will keep the secret, no
living man will ever get the story from me until I lose
my head." Here she is herself to say if I am telling the
truth. "Oh, it's nothing but truth you are telling."

When I saw I was in a man's shape, I said I would
take the child back to his father and mother, as I
knew the grief they were in after him. I got a ship, and
took the child with me; and as I journeyed I came to
land on an island, and I saw not a living soul on it,
only a castle dark and gloomy. I went in to see was

there any one in it. There was no one but an old hag, tall and frightful, and she asked me, "What sort of person are you?" I heard some one groaning in another room, and I said I was a doctor, and I asked her what ailed the person who was groaning.

"Oh," said she, "it is my son, whose hand has been bitten from his wrist by a dog."

I knew then that it was he who had taken the child from me, and I said I would cure him if I got a good reward.

"I have nothing; but there are eight young lads and three young women, as handsome as any one ever laid eyes on, and if you cure him I will give you them."

"Tell me first in what place his hand was cut from him?"

"Oh, it was out in another country, twelve years ago."

"Show me the way, that I may see him."

She brought me into a room, so that I saw him, and his arm was swelled up to the shoulder. He asked me if I would cure him; and I said I would cure him if he would give me the reward his mother promised.

"Oh, I will give it; but cure me."

"Well, bring them out to me."

The hag brought them out of the room. When I looked on her son, he was howling with pain. I said that I would not leave him in pain long. I said to the hag, "He will be howling at first, but will fall asleep presently; do not wake him till he has slept as much as he wants. I will close the door when I am going out." After she went out, I killed the wretch and left the room.

The hag asked me, "Have you given him the cure?"

"Oh, yes; he will sleep for a good while, and I'll come again to have a look at him; but bring me out the young men and the young women."

I took them with me, and I said to her, "Tell me where you got them."

"My son brought them with him, and they are all the children of one king."

I was well satisfied, and I had no wish for delay to get myself free from the hag, so I took them on board the ship, with the child I had myself. I thought the king might leave me the child I nursed myself; but when I came to land, and all those young people with me, the king and queen were out walking. The king was very aged, and the queen aged likewise. When I came to converse with them, and the twelve with me, the king and queen began to cry. I asked, "Why are you crying?"

"It is for good cause I am crying. As many children as these I should have, and now I am withered, grey, at the end of my life, and I have not one at all."

I told him all I went through, and I gave him the child in his hand, and said, "These are your other children who were stolen from you, whom I am giving to you safe. They are gently reared."

When the king heard who they were he smothered them with kisses and drowned them with tears, and dried them with fine cloths silken and the hair of his own head, and so also did their mother, and great was his welcome for me, as it was I who found them all. The king said to me, "I will give you the last child, as it is you who have earned him best; but you must come to my court every year, and the child with you, and I will share with you my possessions.

"I have enough of my own, and after my death I will leave it to the child."

I spent a time, till my visit was over, and I told the king all the troubles I went through, only I said nothing about my wife. And now you have the story.

And now when you go home, and the Slender Red Champion asks you for news of the death of Anshgayliacht and for the sword of light, tell him the way in which the hag's son, his brother, was killed, and say you have the sword; and he will ask the sword from you. Say you to him, "If I promised to bring it to you, I did not promise to give it to you"; and then throw the sword into the air and it will come back to me.

He went home, and he told the story of the death of Anshgayliacht to the Slender Red Champion, "And here," said he, "is the sword." The Slender Red Champion asked for the sword; but he said: "If I promised to bring it to you, I did not promise to give it to you"; and he threw it into the air and it returned to Rough Niall.

The Story of Deirdre

THERE WAS A man in Ireland once who was called Malcolm Harper. The man was a right good man, and he had a goodly share of this world's goods. He had a wife, but no family. What did Malcolm hear but that a soothsayer had come home to the place, and as the man was a right good man, he wished that the soothsayer might come near them. Whether it was that he was invited or that he came of himself, the soothsayer came to the house of Malcolm.

"Are you doing any soothsaying?" says Malcolm.

"Yes, I am doing a little. Are you in need of soothsaying?"

"Well, I do not mind taking soothsaying from you, if you had soothsaying for me, and you would be willing to do it."

"Well, I will do soothsaying for you. What kind of soothsaying do you want?"

"Well, the soothsaying I wanted was that you would tell me my lot or what will happen to me, if you can give me knowledge of it."

"Well, I am going out, and when I return, I will tell you."

And the soothsayer went forth out of the house and he was not long outside when he returned.

41

"Well," said the soothsayer, "I saw in my second sight that it is on account of a daughter of yours that the greatest amount of blood shall be shed that has ever been shed in Erin since time and race began. And the three most famous heroes that ever were found will lose their heads on her account."

After a time a daughter was born to Malcolm, and he did not allow a living being to come to his house, only himself and the nurse. He asked this woman, "Will you yourself bring up the child to keep her in hiding far away where eye will not see a sight of her nor ear hear a word about her?"

The woman said she would, so Malcolm got three men, and he took them away to a large mountain, distant and far from reach, without the knowledge or notice of any one. He caused there a hillock, round the green, to be dug out of the middle, and the hole thus made to be covered carefully over so that a little company could dwell there together. This was done.

Deirdre and her foster-mother dwelt in their bothy [hut] 'mid the hills without the knowledge or the suspicion of any living person about them and without anything occurring, until Deirdre was sixteen years of age. Deirdre grew like the white sapling, straight and trim as the rash [rush] on the moss. She was the creature of fairest form, of loveliest aspect, and of gentlest nature that existed between earth and heaven in all Ireland—whatever colour of hue she had before, there was nobody that looked into her face but she would blush fiery red over it.

The woman that had charge of her, gave Deirdre every information and skill of which she herself had knowledge and skill. There was not a blade of grass growing from root, nor a bird singing in the wood, nor a star shining from heaven but Deirdre had a name for it. But one thing, she did not wish her to have either part or parley with any single living man of the rest of the world. But on a gloomy winter night, with black, scowling clouds, a hunter of game was wearily travelling the hills, and what happened but that he missed the trail of the hunt, and lost his course and companions. A drowsiness came upon the man as he wearily wandered over the hills, and he lay down by the side of the beautiful green knoll in which Deirdre lived, and he slept. The man was faint from hunger and wandering, and benumbed with cold, and a deep sleep fell upon him. When he lay down beside the green hill where Deirdre was, a troubled dream came to the man, and he thought that he enjoyed the warmth of a fairy broch [stone tower], the fairies being inside playing music. The hunter shouted out in his dream, if there was any one in the broch, to let him in for the Holy One's sake. Deirdre heard the voice and said to her foster-mother: "O foster-mother, what cry is that?" "It is nothing at all, Deirdre—merely the birds of the air astray and seeking each other. But let them go past to the bosky [wooded] glade. There is no shelter or house for them here." "Oh, foster-mother, the bird asked to get inside for the sake of the God of the Elements, and you yourself tell me that anything that is asked in His name we ought to do. If you will not allow the bird that is being benumbed with cold, and done to death with hunger, to be let in, I do not think much of your language or your faith. But since I give credence to your language and to your faith, which you taught me, I will myself let in the bird." And Deirdre arose and drew the bolt from the leaf of the door, and she let in the hunter. She placed a seat in the place for sitting, food in the place for eating, and drink in the place for drinking for the man who came to the house. "Oh, for this life and raiment, you man that came in, keep restraint on your tongue!" said the old woman. "It is not a great thing for you to keep your mouth shut and your tongue quiet when you get a home and shelter of a hearth on a gloomy winter's night." "Well," said the hunter, "I may do that—keep my mouth shut and my tongue quiet, since I came to the house and received hospitality from you; but by the hand of thy father and grandfather, and by your own two hands, if some other of the people of the world saw this beauteous creature you have here hid away, they would not long leave her with you, I swear."

"What men are these you refer to?" said Deirdre.

"Well, I will tell you, young woman," said the hunter. "They are Naois, son of Uisnech, and Allen and Arden his two brothers."

"What like are these men when seen, if we were to see them?" said Deirdre.

"Why, the aspect and form of the men when seen

are these," said the hunter: "they have the colour of
the raven on their hair, their skin like swan on the
wave in whiteness, and their cheeks as the blood of
the brindled [streaked] red calf, and their speed and
their leap are those of the salmon of the torrent and
the deer of the grey mountain side. And Naois is head
and shoulders over the rest of the people of Erin."

"However they are," said the nurse, "be you off
from here and take another road. And, King of Light
and Sun! in good sooth and certainty, little are my
thanks for yourself or for her that let you in!"

The hunter went away, and went straight to the
palace of King Connachar. He sent word in to the
king that he wished to speak to him if he pleased.
The king answered the message and came out to
speak to the man. "What is the reason of your journey?" said the king to the hunter.

"I have only to tell you, O king," said the hunter,
"that I saw the fairest creature that ever was born in
Erin, and I came to tell you of it."

"Who is this beauty and where is she to be seen,
when she was not seen before till you saw her, if you
did see her?"

"Well, I did see her," said the hunter. "But, if I did,
no man else can see her unless he get directions
from me as to where she is dwelling."

"And will you direct me to where she dwells? and
the reward of your directing me will be as good as
the reward of your message," said the king.

"Well, I will direct you, O king, although it is likely

that this will not be what they want," said the hunter.

Connachar, King of Ulster, sent for his nearest kinsmen, and he told them of his intent. Though early rose the song of the birds 'mid the rocky caves and the music of the birds in the grove, earlier than that did Connachar, King of Ulster, arise, with his little troop of dear friends, in the delightful twilight of the fresh and gentle May; the dew was heavy on each bush and flower and stem, as they went to bring Deirdre forth from the green knoll where she stayed. Many a youth was there who had a lithe leaping and lissom step when they started whose step was faint, failing, and faltering when they reached the bothy on account of the length of the way and roughness of the road. "Yonder, now, down in the bottom of the glen is the bothy where the woman dwells, but I will not go nearer than this to the old woman," said the hunter.

Connachar with his band of kinsfolk went down to the green knoll where Deirdre dwelt and he knocked at the door of the bothy. The nurse replied, "No less than a king's command and a king's army could put me out of my bothy to-night. And I should be obliged to you, were you to tell who it is that wants me to open my bothy door." "It is I, Connachar, King of Ulster." When the poor woman heard who was at the door, she rose with haste and let in the king and all that could get in of his retinue.

When the king saw the woman that was before him that he had been in quest of, he thought he never saw in the course of the day nor in the dream of night a creature so fair as Deirdre and he gave his full heart's weight of love to her. Deirdre was raised on the topmost of the heroes' shoulders and she and her foster-mother were brought to the Court of King Connachar of Ulster.

With the love that Connachar had for her, he wanted to marry Deirdre right off there and then, will she nill she marry him. But she said to him, "I would be obliged to you if you will give me the respite of a year and a day." He said, "I will grant you that, hard though it is, if you will give me your unfailing promise that you will marry me at the year's end." And she gave the promise. Connachar got for her a woman-teacher and merry modest maidens fair that would lie down and rise with her, that would play and speak with her. Deirdre was clever in maidenly duties and wifely understanding, and Connacher thought he never saw with bodily eye a creature that pleased him more.

Deirdre and her women companions were one day out on the hillock behind the house enjoying the scene, and drinking in the sun's heat. What did they see coming but three men a-journeying. Deirdre was looking at the men that were coming, and wondering at them. When the men neared them, Deirdre remembered the language of the huntsman, and she said to herself that these were the three sons of Uisnech—Naois, Arden, and Allen. The three brothers went past without taking any notice of them, without even glancing at the young girls on the hillock. What

happened but that love for Naois struck the heart of
Deirdre, so that she could not but follow after him.
She girded up her raiment and went after the men
that went past the base of the knoll, leaving her
women attendants there. Allen and Arden had heard
of the woman that Connacher, King of Ulster, had
with him, and they thought that, if Naois, their brother,
saw her, he would have her himself, more especially
as she was not married to the king. They perceived
the woman coming, and called on one another to
hasten their step as they had a long distance to travel,
and the dusk of night was coming on. They did so.
She cried: "Naois, son of Uisnech, will you leave me?"
"What piercing, shrill cry is that—the most melodious
my ear ever heard, and the shrillest that ever struck
my heart of all the cries I ever heard?" "It is nothing
but the wail of the wave-swans of Connachar," said
his brothers. "No! yonder is a woman's cry of dis-
tress," said Naois, and he swore he would not go
further until he saw from whom the cry came, and
Naois turned back. Naois and Deirdre met, and
Deirdre kissed Naois three times, and a kiss each to
his brothers. With the confusion that she was in,
Deirdre went into a crimson blaze of fire, and her
colour came and went as rapidly as the movement of
the aspen by the stream side. Naois thought he never
saw a fairer creature, and Naois gave Deirdre the love
that he never gave to thing, to vision, or to creature
but to herself.

Then Naois placed Deirdre on the topmost height
of his shoulders, and told his brothers to keep up their

Then Naois placed Deirdre on the topmost height of his shoulders, and told his brothers to keep up their pace.

pace, and they kept up their pace. Naois thought that it would not be well for him to remain in Erin on account of the way in which Connacher, King of Ulster, his uncle's son, had gone against him because of the woman, though he had not married her; and he turned back to Alba, that is, Scotland. He reached the side of Loch-Ness and made his habitation there. He could kill the salmon of the torrent from out his own door, and the deer of the grey gorge from out his window. Naois and Deirdre and Allen and Arden dwelt in a tower, and they were happy so long a time as they were there.

By this time the end of the period came at which Deirdre had to marry Connachar, King of Ulster. Connachar made up his mind to take Deirdre away by the sword whether she was married to Naois or not. So he prepared a great and gleeful feast. He sent word far and wide through Erin all to his kinspeople to come to the feast. Connachar thought to himself that Naois would not come though he should bid him; and the scheme that arose in his mind was to send for his father's brother, Ferchar Mac Ro, and to send him on an embassy to Naois. He did so; and Connachar said to Ferchar, "Tell Naois, son of Uisnech, that I am setting forth a great and gleeful feast to my friends and kinspeople throughout the wide extent of Erin all, and that I shall not have rest by day nor sleep by night if he and Allen and Arden be not partakers of the feast."

Ferchar Mac Ro and his three sons went on their

journey, and reached the tower where Naois was dwelling by the side of Loch-Ness. The sons of Uisnech gave a cordial kindly welcome to Ferchar Mac Ro and his three sons, and asked of him the news of Erin. "The best news that I have for you," said the hardy hero, "is that Connachar, King of Ulster, is setting forth a great sumptuous feast to his friends and kinspeople throughout the wide extent of Erin all, and he has vowed by the earth beneath him, by the high heaven above him, and by the sun that wends to the west, that he will have no rest by day nor sleep by night if the sons of Uisnech, the sons of his own father's brother, will not come back to the land of their home and the soil of their nativity, and to the feast likewise, and he has sent us on embassy to invite you."

"We will go with you," said Naois.

"We will," said his brothers.

But Deirdre did not wish to go with Ferchar Mac Ro, and she tried every prayer to turn Naois from going with him—she said:

"I saw a vision, Naois, and do you interpret it to me," said Deirdre—then she sang:

> O Naois, son of Uisnech, hear
>   What was shown in a dream to me.
>
> There came three white doves out of the South
>   Flying over the sea,
> And drops of honey were in their mouth
>   From the hive of the honey-bee.

> O Naois, son of Uisnech, hear,
> What was shown in a dream to me.

> I saw three grey hawks out of the south
> Come flying over the sea,
> And the red red drops they bare in their mouth
> They were dearer than life to me.

Said Naois:—

> It is nought but the fear of woman's heart,
> And a dream of the night, Deirdre.

"The day that Connachar sent the invitation to his feast will be unlucky for us if we don't go, O Deirdre."

"You will go there," said Ferchar Mac Ro; "and if Connachar show kindness to you, show ye kindness to him; and if he will display wrath towards you display ye wrath towards him, and I and my three sons will be with you."

"We will," said Daring Drop. "We will," said Hardy Holly. "We will," said Fiallan the Fair.

"I have three sons, and they are three heroes, and in any harm or danger that may befall you, they will be with you, and I myself will be along with them." And Ferchar Mac Ro gave his vow and his word in presence of his arms that, in any harm or danger that came in the way of the sons of Uisnech, he and his three sons would not leave head on live body in Erin, despite sword or helmet, spear or shield, blade or mail, be they ever so good.

Deirdre was unwilling to leave Alba, but she went

with Naois. Deirdre wept tears in showers and she
sang:

> Dear is the land, the land over there,
>> Alba full of woods and lakes;
> Bitter to my heart is leaving thee,
>> But I go away with Naois.

Ferchar Mac Ro did not stop till he got the sons of
Uisnech away with him, despite the suspicion of
Deirdre.

> The coracle [small boat] was put to sea,
>> The sail was hoisted to it;
> And the second morrow they arrived
>> On the white shores of Erin.

As soon as the sons of Uisnech landed in Erin,
Ferchar Mac Ro sent word to Connachar, king of
Ulster, that the men whom he wanted were come,
and let him now show kindness to them. "Well," said
Connachar, "I did not expect that the sons of Uisnech
would come, though I sent for them, and I am not
quite ready to receive them. But there is a house
down yonder where I keep strangers, and let them go
down to it to-day, and my house will be ready before
them to-morrow."

But he that was up in the palace felt it long that he
was not getting word as to how matters were going
on for those down in the house of the strangers. "Go
you, Gelban Grednach, son of Lochlin's king, go you

down and bring me information as to whether her former hue and complexion are on Deirdre. If they be, I will take her out with edge of blade and point of sword, and if not, let Naois, son of Uisnech, haver her for himself," said Connachar.

Gelban, the cheering and charming son of Lochlin's king, went down to the place of the strangers, where the sons of Uisnech and Deirdre were staying. He looked in through the bicker-hole on the door-leaf. Now she that he gazed upon used to go into a crimson blaze of blushes when any one looked at her. Naois looked at Deirdre and knew that some one was looking at her from the back of the door-leaf. He rose up and flung open the door, and he knocked down Gelban Grednach the Cheerful and Charming, son of Lochlin's king. Gelban returned back to the palace of King Connachar.

"You were cheerful, charming, going away, but you are cheerless, charmless, returning. What has happened to you, Gelban? But have you seen her, and are Deirdre's hue and complexion as before?" said Connachar.

"Well, I have seen Deirdre, and I saw her also truly, and while I was looking at her through the bicker-hole on the door, Naois, son of Uisnech, knocked me down. But of a truth and verity, although he knocked me down, it were my desire still to remain looking at her, were it not for the hurry you told me to be in," said Gelban.

"That is true," said Connachar; "let three hundred

brave heroes go down to the abode of the strangers, and let them bring hither to me Deirdre, and kill the rest."

Connachar ordered three hundred heroes to go down to the abode of the strangers and to take Deirdre up with them and kill the rest. "The pursuit is coming," said Deirdre.

"Yes, but I will myself go out and stop the pursuit," said Naois.

"It is not you, but we that will go," said Daring Drop, and Hardy Holly, and Fiallan the Fair; "it is to us that our father entrusted your defence from harm and danger when he himself left for home." And the gallant youths, full noble, full manly, full handsome, with beauteous brown locks, went forth girt with battle arms fit for fierce fight and clothed with combat dress for fierce contest fit, which was burnished, bright, brilliant, bladed, blazing, on which were many pictures of beasts and birds and creeping things, lions and lithe-limbed tigers, brown eagle and harrying hawk and adder fierce; and the young heroes laid low three-thirds of the company.

Connachar came out in haste and cried with wrath: "Who is there on the floor of fight, slaughtering my men?"

"We, the three sons of Ferchar Mac Ro."

"Well," said the king, "I will give a free bridge to your grandfather, a free bridge to your father, and a free bridge each to you three brothers, if you come over to my side to-night."

"Well, Connachar, we will not accept that offer from you nor thank you for it. Greater by far do we prefer to go home to our father and tell the deeds of heroism we have done, than accept anything on these terms from you. Naois, son of Uisnech, and Allen and Arden are as nearly related to yourself as they are to us, though you are so keen to shed their blood, and you would shed our blood also, Connachar." And the noble, manly, handsome youths with beauteous, brown locks returned to Naois. "We are now," said they, "going home to tell our father that you are now safe from the hands of the king." And the youths all fresh and tall and lithe and beautiful, went home to their father to tell that the sons of Uisnech were safe. This happened at the parting of the day and night in the morning twilight time, and Naois said they must go away, leave that house, and return to Alba.

Naois and Deirdre, Allan and Arden started to return to Alba. Word came to the king that the company he was in pursuit of were gone. The king then sent for Duanan Gacha Druid, the best magician he had, and he spoke to him as follows:—"Much wealth have I expended on you, Duanan Gacha Druid, to give schooling and learning and magic mystery to you, if these people get away from me to-day without care, without consideration or regard for me, without chance of overtaking them, and without power to stop them."

"Well, I will stop them," said the magician, "until the company you send in pursuit return." And the magician placed a wood before them through which no man could go, but the sons of Uisnech marched through the wood without halt or hesitation, and Deirdre held on to Naois's hand.

"What is the good of that? that will not do yet," said Connachar. "They are off without bending of their feet or stopping of their step, without heed or respect to me, and I am without power to keep up to them or opportunity to turn them back this night."

"I will try another plan on them," said the druid; and he placed before them a grey sea instead of a green plain. The three heroes stripped and tied their clothes behind their heads, and Naois placed Deirdre on the top of his shoulder.

> They stretched their sides to the stream,
>   And sea and land were to them the same,
> The rough grey ocean was the same
>   As meadow-land green and plain.

"Though that be good, O Duanan, it will not make the heroes return," said Connachar; "they are gone without regard for me, and without honour to me, and without power on my part to pursue them or to force them to return this night."

"We shall try another method on them, since yon one did not stop them," said the druid. And the druid froze the grey ridged sea into hard rocky knobs, the sharpness of sword being on the one edge and the poison power of adders on the other. Then Arden cried that he was getting tired, and nearly giving over. "Come you, Arden, and sit on my right shoulder," said Naois. Arden came and sat on Naois's shoulder. Arden was long in this posture when he died; but though he was dead Naois would not let him go. Allen then cried out that he was getting faint and nigh-well giving up. When Naois heard his prayer, he gave forth the piercing sigh of death, and asked Allen to lay hold of him and he would bring him to land. Allen was not long when the weakness of death came on him and his hold failed. Naois looked around, and when he saw his two well-beloved brothers dead, he cared not whether he lived or died, and he gave forth the bitter sigh of death, and his heart burst.

"They are gone," said Duanan Gacha Druid to the king, "and I have done what you desired me. The sons of Uisnech are dead and they will trouble you no more; and you have your wife hale and whole to yourself."

"Blessings for that upon you and may the good results accrue to me, Duanan. I count it no loss what I spent in the schooling and teaching of you. Now dry up the flood, and let me see if I can behold Deirdre," said Connachar. And Duanan Gacha Druid dried up the flood from the plain and the three sons of Uisnech were lying together dead, without breath of life, side by side on the green meadow plain and Deirdre bending above showering down her tears.

Then Deirdre said this lament: "Fair one, loved one, flower of beauty; beloved upright and strong; beloved noble and modest warrior. Fair one, blue-eyed, beloved of thy wife; lovely to me at the trysting-place came thy clear voice through the woods of Ireland. I cannot eat or smile henceforth. Break not to-day, my heart: soon enough shall I lie within my grave. Strong are the waves of sorrow, but stronger is sorrow's self, Connachar."

The people then gathered round the heroes' bodies and asked Connachar what was to be done with the bodies. The order that he gave was that they should dig a pit and put the three brothers in it side by side.

Deirdre kept sitting on the brink of the grave, constantly asking the gravediggers to dig the pit wide and free. When the bodies of the brothers were put in the grave, Deirdre said:—

> Come over hither, Naois, my love,
> Let Arden close to Allen lie;
> If the dead had any sense to feel,
> Ye would have made a place for Deirdre.

The men did as she told them. She jumped into the grave and lay down by Naois, and she was dead by his side.

The king ordered the body to be raised from out the grave and to be buried on the other side of the loch. It was done as the king bade, and the pit closed. Thereupon a fir shoot grew out of the grave of Deirdre and a fir shoot from the grave of Naois, and the two shoots united in a knot above the loch. The king ordered the shoots to be cut down, and this was done twice, until, at the third time, the wife whom the king had married caused him to stop this work of evil and his vengeance on the remains of the dead.

The Llanfabon Changeling

AT A FARMHOUSE called Berth Gron, in the parish of Llanfabon, there once lived a young widow. She had a little boy whom she loved more than her own eyes. He was her only comfort, and she was afraid of letting the sun shine on him, as the saying goes. Pryderi—that was the name she had given him—was about three years old, and a fine child for his age.

At this time the parish of Llanfabon was full of fairies. On nights when the moon was bright, they often used to keep the hard-working farmers awake with their music until the cock crew in the morning. On nights when the moon was dark, they delighted in luring men into desolate bogs by displaying false lights. Even in the daytime they would play tricks on people if they were not very careful.

The widow knew that the Fair Family were very fond of stealing babies out of their cradles, and you can imagine how careful she was of her little treasure. She hated leaving him out of her sight by night or day: if ever she had to do so, she was miserable until she returned to him and found him safe and sound.

One day when he was lying asleep in his cradle, she heard the cows in the byre lowing piteously as if

61

they were in great pain. As there was nobody in the house but herself to look after her precious boy, she was afraid at first of going out to see what was amiss. The lowing, however, became more and more agonised, and she became frightened. Not being able to stand it any longer, she rushed out, forgetting in her fright to place the tongs crossways on the cradle.

When she got to the cow house, she was amazed to find that there was nothing whatever the matter with the cattle: they were chewing their cud placidly, and they turned their great meek eyes in mild surprise upon her, evidently wondering why she had burst in upon them so unceremoniously. Realising that she had been the victim of some deception, she ran back to the house as fast as her feet could carry her, and to the cradle. She was afraid of finding it empty, but bending over it she found a little boy in it who greeted her with "Mother." She looked hard at him: he was very like Pryderi, and yet there was a something about him which made her think that he was different from him. At last she said doubtingly, "You are not my child."

"I am truly," said the little one. "What do you mean, mother?"

But something kept whispering to her constantly that he was not her child, and as time went on she became convinced that she was right. The little boy after a while became cross and fretful, unlike Pryderi, who was always as good as gold. In a whole year he never grew at all.

Pryderi, on the other hand, was a very growing child. Besides, the little fellow seemed to get uglier every day, whereas Pryderi had been getting prettier and prettier: at least his mother thought so. She did not know what to do.

Now, there was in the parish of Llanfabon a man who had the reputation of being well informed on matters which are dark to most people. This reputation he had gained by living at a place called the Castle of the Night. This castle had been built of stones from Llanfabon Church, and was haunted. Many men had tried to live there, but had been compelled to leave because ghosts plagued them so. That this man was able to dwell there in seeming peace and comfort was proof positive, in the eyes of the people of Llanfabon, that he had some control at least over the powers of darkness.

The widow went to this wise man and laid her trouble before him. After hearing her story he said to her, "If you follow my directions faithfully and minutely, I think I shall be able to help you. At noon to-morrow take an eggshell and prepare to brew some beer in it. See that the boy watches what you are doing, but take care not to tell him to pay attention. He will ask you what you are doing. You are to say, 'I am brewing beer for the harvestmen.' Listen carefully to what he says when he hears that, but pretend not to catch it. After you have put him to bed to-morrow night, come and tell me all about it."

The widow returned home, and the next day at

noon she followed the cunning man's advice. She took an eggshell and got everything ready for brewing beer. The boy stood by her, watching her as a cat watches a mouse. Presently he asked, "What are you doing, mother?" She said, "I am brewing beer for the harvestmen, my boy." Then the boy said quietly to himself:

> "I am very old this day,
> I was living before my birth,
> I remember yonder oak
> An acorn in the earth,
> But I never saw the egg of a hen
> Brewing beer for harvestmen."

The widow heard what he said, but pretended not to have caught it, and asked, "What did you say, my son?" He said, "Nothing, mother." She then turned round and saw that he was very cross, and the angry expression on his face made him very repulsive to look upon.

After she had put him to bed that night, the widow went to the Castle of the Night, as she had been ordered. As soon as she entered, the wise man asked, "Were you able to catch what he said?"

"He spoke very quietly to himself," answered the widow, "but I am quite sure that what he said was:

> 'I am very old this day,
> I was living before my birth,
> I remember yonder oak

An acorn in the earth,
But I never saw the egg of a hen
Brewing beer for harvestmen.'"

"It is well," said the wise man. "If you follow my directions faithfully and minutely, I think I shall be able to help you. The moon will be full in four days, and you must go at midnight to where the four roads meet above the Ford of the Bell. Hide yourself somewhere where you can see everything that comes along any of the roads without being seen yourself. Whatever happens, do not stir or utter a sound. If you do, my plans will be frustrated and your own life will be in danger. Come to me the day after and tell me what you see."

By midnight on the appointed day the widow had concealed herself carefully behind a large bush near the cross-roads above the Ford of the Bell, where she could see everything that came along any of the four roads without being seen herself. For a long time there was nothing to be seen or heard: the moon shone brightly, and the melancholy silence of midnight lay over all. Before long dark clouds obscured the moon, and at last the anxious widow heard the faint sounds of music in the far distance. The strains came nearer and nearer, and she listened with rapt attention. Before long the melody was close at hand, and she saw a procession of fairies coming along one of the roads. Soon the vanguard of the procession came up, and she saw that there were hun-

dreds of fairies marching along. They were singing
the sweetest songs she had ever heard, and she felt
that she could listen to them for ever. Just as the
middle of the procession came opposite her hiding
place, the moon emerged from behind a black cloud,
and in the clear, cold light which then flooded the
earth she beheld a sight which turned her pleasure
into bitter pain and made her heart beat almost out of
her body. Walking between two fairies was her own
dear little boy. She nearly forgot herself altogether,
and was on the point of springing into the midst of
the fairies to snatch her darling from them. But she
remembered in time that the wise man had warned
her that his plans would be upset and her own life in
danger if she carried out her intention, and con-
trolling herself by a supreme effort she neither stirred
nor uttered a sound. When the long procession had
wound itself past and the music had died away in the
distance, she issued from her concealment and went
home to bed, but her heart was so full of longing for
her lost child that she never slept a wink all night.

On the morrow she went to the wise man early. He
was expecting her, and as she entered he perceived
by her looks that she had seen something to disturb
her. She told him what she had witnessed at the
cross-roads, and he again said, "It is well. If you will
follow my directions faithfully and minutely, I think I
shall be able to help you."

He then brought out a great book, bound in calf-
skin, opened it, and pored long over it. After much

Walking between two fairies was her own dear little boy.

deliberation he said, "You must find a black hen without a single white feather, or one of any other colour than black. Do you burn peat or wood?"

"I burn peat," said the widow.

"After you have found the hen," resumed the wise man, "you must light a wood fire and bake the hen before it, with its feathers and all intact. After you have placed it to bake before the fire, close every passage and hole in the wall, leaving only the chimney open. After that, avoid looking at the boy, but watch the hen baking, and do not take your eyes off it until the last feather has fallen off it."

Strange as the directions of the wise man appeared, she determined to follow them as faithfully and minutely as she had the previous directions. But oh, the weary tramp she had before she could find a black hen without a single white feather or one of any other colour than black. She tried every farm in the parish of Llanfabon in vain, and she was nearly driven to the conclusion that if this breed of hens had ever existed on the earth it had become extinct. It was weeks before she secured the right hen, and it was at a farm miles away from Llanfabon that she was successful in her search.

Her repeated disappointments were all the more bitter because she was forced to hide her disgust with the little fellow who was there instead of her boy. When he addressed her as "Mother," it was almost more than she could bear, but she was just able to make no difference in her behaviour towards him, though he seemed to be getting smaller, crosser and uglier every day.

Having found the black hen, she built up a wood fire, and when it was burning brightly she wrung the hen's neck and placed it as it was, feathers and all, in front of the fire. She then closed every passage and hole in the walls, leaving only the chimney open, and sat in front of the fire to watch the hen baking. The little fellow called to her several times, but though she answered him she was careful not to look at him. After a bit she fell into a swoon. When she came out of it she saw that all the feathers had fallen off the hen, and looking round the house she saw that the changeling had disappeared. Then she heard the strains of music outside the house, and they were the same as those she had heard at the cross-roads. All of a sudden the music ceased, and she heard a little boy's voice calling, "Mother." She rushed out, and lo! and behold, who should be standing within a few paces of the threshold but her own dear little boy. She snatched him up in her arms and almost smothered him with kisses. She laughed and wept in turn, and her joy was greater than words can tell. When asked where he had been all this long while, the little boy had no account to give of himself except that he had been listening to lovely music. He was pale and wan and thin, but under his mother's loving care he soon became his bonny self again, and mother and son lived happily ever afterwards.

Beth Gellert

PRINCE LLEWELYN had a favourite greyhound named Gellert that had been given to him by his father-in-law, King John. He was as gentle as a lamb at home but a lion in the chase. One day Llewelyn went to the chase and blew his horn in front of his castle. All his other dogs came to the call but Gellert never answered it. So he blew a louder blast on his horn and called Gellert by name, but still the greyhound did not come. At last Prince Llewelyn could wait no longer and went off to the hunt without Gellert. He had little sport that day because Gellert was not there, the swiftest and boldest of his hounds.

He turned back in a rage to his castle, and as he came to the gate, who should he see but Gellert come bounding out to meet him. But when the hound came near him, the Prince was startled to see that his lips and fangs were dripping with blood. Llewelyn started back and the greyhound crouched down at his feet as if surprised or afraid at the way his master greeted him.

Now Prince Llewelyn had a little son a year old with whom Gellert used to play, and a terrible thought crossed the Prince's mind that made him rush towards the child's nursery. And the nearer he came the more blood and disorder he found about the rooms. He rushed into it and found the child's cradle overturned and daubed with blood.

Prince Llewelyn grew more and more terrified, and sought for his little son everywhere. He could find him nowhere but only signs of some terrible conflict in which much blood had been shed. At last he felt sure the dog had destroyed his child, and shouting to Gellert, "Monster, thou hast devoured my child," he drew out his sword and plunged it in the greyhound's side, who fell with a deep yell and still gazing in his master's eyes.

As Gellert raised his dying yell, a little child's cry answered it from beneath the cradle, and there Llewelyn found his child unharmed and just awakened from sleep. But just beside him lay the body of a great gaunt wolf all torn to pieces and covered with blood. Too late, Llewelyn learned what had happened while he was away. Gellert had stayed behind to guard the child and had fought and slain the wolf that had tried to destroy Llewelyn's heir.

In vain was all Llewelyn's grief; he could not bring his faithful dog to life again. So he buried him outside the castle walls within sight of the great mountain of Snowdon, where every passer-by might see his grave, and raised over it a great cairn of stones. And to this day the place is called Beth Gellert, or the Grave of Gellert.

The Sea-Maiden

THERE WAS ONCE a poor old fisherman, and one year he was not getting much fish. On a day of days, while he was fishing, there rose a sea-maiden at the side of his boat, and she asked him, "Are you getting much fish?" The old man answered and said, "Not I." "What reward would you give me for sending plenty of fish to you?" "Ach!" said the old man, "I have not much to spare." "Will you give me the first son you have?" said she. "I would give ye that, were I to have a son," said he. "Then go home, and remember me when your son is twenty years of age, and you yourself will get plenty of fish after this." Everything happened as the sea-maiden said, and he himself got plenty of fish; but when the end of the twenty years was nearing, the old man was growing more and more sorrowful and heavy hearted, while he counted each day as it came.

He had rest neither day nor night. The son asked his father one day, "Is any one troubling you?" The old man said, "Some one is, but that's nought to do with you nor any one else." The lad said, "I *must* know what it is." His father told him at last how the matter was with him and the sea-maiden. "Let not that put you in any trouble," said the son; "I will not oppose you." "You shall not; you shall not go, my son, though I never get fish any more." "If you will not let me go with you, go to the smithy, and let the smith make me a great strong sword, and I will go seek my fortune."

His father went to the smithy, and the smith made a doughty sword for him. His father came home with the sword. The lad grasped it and gave it a shake or two, and it flew into a hundred splinters. He asked his father to go to the smithy and get him another sword in which there should be twice as much weight; and so his father did, and so likewise it happened to the next sword—it broke in two halves. Back went the old man to the smithy; and the smith made a great sword, its like he never made before. "There's thy sword for thee," said the smith, "and the fist must be good that plays this blade." The old man gave the sword to his son; he gave it a shake or two. "This will do," said he; "it's high time now to travel on my way."

On the next morning he put a saddle on a black horse that his father had, and he took the world for his pillow. When he went on a bit, he fell in with the carcass of a sheep beside the road. And there were a great black dog, a falcon, and an otter, and they were quarrelling over the spoil. So they asked him to divide it for them. He came down off the horse, and he divided the carcass amongst the three. Three shares to the dog, two shares to the otter, and a share to the falcon. "For this," said the dog, "if swiftness of foot or

sharpness of tooth will give thee aid, mind me, and I
will be at thy side." Said the otter, "If the swimming of
foot on the ground of a pool will loose thee, mind
me, and I will be at thy side." Said the falcon, "If
hardship comes on thee, where swiftness of wing or
crook of a claw will do good, mind me, and I will be
at thy side."

On this he went onward till he reached a king's
house, and he took service to be a herd, and his
wages were to be according to the milk of the cattle.
He went away with the cattle, and the grazing was but
bare. In the evening when he took them home they
had not much milk, the place was so bare, and his
meat and drink was but spare that night.

On the next day he went on further with them; and
at last he came to a place exceedingly grassy, in a
green glen, of which he never saw the like.

But about the time when he should drive the cattle
homewards, who should he see coming but a great
giant with his sword in his hand? "HI! HO! HOGARAICH!!!"
says the giant. "Those cattle are mine; they are on my
land, and a dead man art thou." "I say not that," says
the herd; "there is no knowing, but that may be easier
to say than to do."

He drew the great clean-sweeping sword, and he
neared the giant. The herd drew back his sword, and
the head was off the giant in a twinkling. He leaped
on the black horse, and he went to look for the
giant's house. In went the herd, and that's the place
where there was money in plenty, and dresses of

each kind in the wardrobe with gold and silver, and each thing finer than the other. At the mouth of night he took himself to the king's house, but he took not a thing from the giant's house. And when the cattle were milked this night there *was* milk. He got good feeding this night, meat and drink without stint, and the king was hugely pleased that he had caught such a herd. He went on for a time in this way, but at last the glen grew bare of grass, and the grazing was not so good.

So he thought he would go a little further forward in on the giant's land; and he sees a great park of grass. He returned for the cattle, and he put them into the park.

They were but a short time grazing in the park when a great wild giant came full of rage and madness. "HI! HAW!! HOGARAICH!!!" said the giant. "It is a drink of thy blood that will quench my thirst this night." "There is no knowing," said the herd, "but that's easier to say than to do." And at each other went the men. *There* was shaking of blades! At length and at last it seemed as if the giant would get the victory over the herd. Then he called on his dog, and with one spring the animal caught the giant by the neck, and swiftly the herd struck off his head.

He went home very tired this night, but it's a wonder if the king's cattle had not milk. The whole family was delighted that they had got such a herd.

Next day he betakes himself to the castle. When he reached the door, a little flattering carlin [old woman] met him standing in the door. "All hail and good luck to thee, fisher's son; 'tis I myself am pleased to see thee; great is the honour for this kingdom, for thy like to be come into it—thy coming in is fame for this little bothy; go in first; honour to the gentles; go on, and take breath."

"In before me, thou crone; I like not flattery out of doors; go in and let's hear thy speech." In went the crone, and when her back was to him he drew his sword and whips her head off; but the sword flew out of his hand. And swift the crone gripped her head with both hands, and puts it on her neck as it was before. The herd's dog sprung on the crone, and she struck the generous dog with the club of magic; and there he lay. But the herd struggled for a hold of the club of magic, and with one blow on the top of the head she was on earth in the twinkling of an eye. He went forward, up a little, and there was spoil! Gold and silver, and each thing more precious than another, in the crone's castle. He went back to the king's house, and then there was rejoicing.

He followed herding in this way for a time; but one night after he came home, instead of getting "All hail" and "Good luck" from the dairymaid, all were at crying and woe.

He asked what cause of woe there was that night. The dairymaid said "There is a great beast with three heads in the loch, and it must get some one every year, and the lot had come this year on the king's daughter, and at midday to-morrow she is to meet the

Laidly [ugly, repulsive] Beast at the upper end of the loch, but there is a great suitor yonder who is going to rescue her."

"What suitor is that?" said the herd. "Oh, he is a great General of arms," said the dairymaid, "and when he kills the beast, he will marry the king's daughter, for the king has said that he who could save his daughter should get her to marry."

But on the morrow, when the time grew near, the king's daughter and this hero of arms went to give a meeting to the beast, and they reached the black rock, at the upper end of the loch. They were but a short time there when the beast stirred in the midst of the loch; but when the General saw this terror of a beast with three heads, he took fright, and he slunk away, and he hid himself. And the king's daughter was under fear and under trembling, with no one at all to save her. Suddenly she sees a doughty [valiant] handsome youth, riding a black horse, and coming where she was. He was marvellously arrayed and full armed, and his dog moved after him. "There is gloom on your face, girl," said the youth; "what do you here?"

"Oh! that's no matter," said the king's daughter. "It's not long I'll be here, at all events."

"I say not that," said he.

"A champion fled as likely as you, and not long since," said she.

"He is a champion who stands the war," said the youth. And to meet the beast he went with his sword and his dog. But there was a spluttering and a splashing between himself and the beast! The dog kept doing all he might, and the king's daughter was palsied by fear of the noise of the beast! One of them would now be under, and now above. But at last he cut one of the heads off it. It gave one roar, and the son of earth, echo of the rocks, called to its screech, and it drove the loch in spindrift from end to end, and in a twinkling it went out of sight.

"Good luck and victory follow you, lad!" said the king's daughter. "I am safe for one night, but the beast will come again and again, until the other two heads come off it." He caught the beast's head, and he drew a knot through it, and he told her to bring it with her there to-morrow. She gave him a gold ring, and went home with the head on her shoulder, and the herd betook himself to the cows. But she had not gone far when this great General saw her, and he said to her, "I will kill you if you do not say that 'twas I took the head off the beast." "Oh!" says she, "'tis I will say it; who else took the head off the beast but you!" They reached the king's house, and the head was on the General's shoulder. But here was rejoicing, that she should come home alive and whole, and this great captain with the beast's head full of blood in his hand. On the morrow they went away, and there was no question at all but that this hero would save the king's daughter.

They reached the same place, and they were not long there when the fearful Laidly Beast stirred in the midst of the loch, and the hero slunk away as he did on yesterday, but it was not long after this when the man of the black horse came, with another dress on. No matter; she knew that it was the very same lad. "It is I am pleased to see you," said she. "I am in hopes you will handle your great sword to-day as you did yesterday. Come up and take breath." But they were not long there when they saw the beast steaming in the midst of the loch.

At once he went to meet the beast, but *there* was Cloopersteich and Claperstich, spluttering, splashing, raving, and roaring on the beast! They kept at it thus for a long time, and about the mouth of night he cut another head off the beast. He put it on the knot and gave it to her. She gave him one of her earrings, and he leaped on the black horse, and he betook himself to the herding. The king's daughter went home with the heads. The General met her, and took the heads from her, and he said to her, that she must tell that it was he who took the head off the beast this time also. "Who else took the head off the beast but you?" said she. They reached the king's house with the heads. Then there was joy and gladness.

About the same time on the morrow, the two went away. The officer hid himself as he usually did. The king's daughter betook herself to the bank of the loch. The hero of the black horse came, and if roaring and raving were on the beast on the days that were passed, this day it was horrible. But no matter, he took the third head off the beast, and drew it through the knot, and gave it to her. She gave him her other earring, and then she went home with the heads. When they reached the king's house, all were full of smiles, and the General was to marry the king's daughter the next day. The wedding was going on, and every one about the castle longing till the priest should come. But when the priest came, she would marry only the one who could take the heads off the knot without cutting it. "Who should take the heads off the knot but the man that put the heads on?" said the king.

The General tried them, but he could not loose them, and at last there was no one about the house but had tried to take the heads off the knot, but they could not. The king asked if there were any one else about the house that would try to take the heads off the knot. They said that the herd had not tried them yet. Word went for the herd; and he was not long throwing them hither and thither. "But stop a bit, my lad," said the king's daughter; "the man that took the heads off the beast, he has my ring and my two earrings." The herd put his hand in his pocket, and he threw them on the board. "Thou art my man," said the king's daughter. The king was not so pleased when he saw that it was a herd who was to marry his daughter, but he ordered that he should be put in a better dress; but his daughter spoke, and she said that he had a dress as fine as any that ever was in his castle; and thus it happened. The herd put on the giant's golden dress, and they married that same day.

They were now married, and everything went on well. But one day, and it was the namesake of the day when his father had promised him to the sea-maiden, they were sauntering by the side of the loch, and lo and behold! she came and took him away to the loch without leave or asking. The king's daughter was now mournful, tearful, blind-sorrowful for her married man; she was always with her eye on the loch. An old soothsayer met her, and she told how it had befallen her married mate. Then he told her the thing to do to save her mate, and that she did.

She took her harp to the sea-shore, and sat and played; and the sea-maiden came up to listen, for sea-maidens are fonder of music than all other creatures. But when the wife saw the sea-maiden she stopped. The sea-maiden said, "Play on!" but the princess said, "No, not till I see my man again." So the sea-maiden put up his head out of the loch. Then the princess played again, and stopped till the sea-maiden put him up to the waist. Then the princess played and stopped again, and this time the sea-maiden put him all out of the loch, and he called on the falcon and became one and flew to shore. But the sea-maiden took the princess, his wife.

Sorrowful was each one that was in the town on this night. Her man was mournful, tearful, wandering down and up about the banks of the loch, by day and night. The old soothsayer met him. The soothsayer told him that there was no way of killing the sea-maiden but the one way, and this is it—"In the island

*She took her harp to the sea-shore, and sat and played;
and the sea-maiden came up to listen, for sea-maidens
are fonder of music than all other creatures.*

that is in the midst of the loch is the white-footed hind [deer] of the slenderest legs and the swiftest step, and though she be caught, there will spring a hoodie [crow] out of her, and though the hoodie should be caught, there will spring a trout out of her, but there is an egg in the mouth of the trout, and the soul of the sea-maiden is in the egg, and if the egg breaks, she is dead."

Now, there was no way of getting to this island, for the sea-maiden would sink each boat and raft that would go on the loch. He thought he would try to leap the strait with the black horse, and even so he did. The black horse leaped the strait. He saw the hind, and he let his dog after her, but when he was on one side of the island, the hind would be on the other side. "Oh! would the black dog of the carcass of flesh were here!" No sooner spoke he the word than that grateful dog was at his side; and after the hind he went, and they were not long in bringing her to earth. But he no sooner caught her than a hoodie sprang out of her. "Would that the falcon grey, of sharpest eye and swiftest wing, were here!" No sooner said he this than the falcon was after the hoodie, and she was not long putting her to earth; and as the hoodie fell on the bank of the loch, out of her jumps the trout. "Oh! that thou wert by me now, oh otter!" No sooner said than the otter was at his side, and out on the loch she leaped, and brings the trout from the midst of the loch; but no sooner was the otter on shore with the trout than the egg came from its mouth. He sprang and he put his foot on it. 'Twas then the sea-maiden appeared, and she said, "Break not the egg, and you shall get all you ask." "Deliver to me my wife!" In the wink of an eye she was by his side. When he got hold of her hand in both his hands, he let his foot down on the egg, and the sea-maiden died.

CHILDREN'S THRIFT CLASSICS

Just $1.00
All books complete and unabridged, except where noted.
96pp., 5³⁄₁₆″ × 8¹⁄₄″, paperbound.